Ernie and Hermie visit Earth

Level 3G

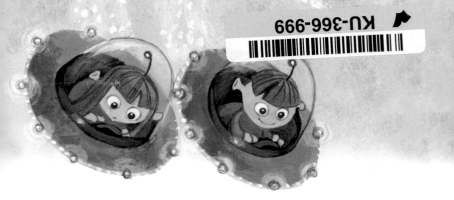

Written by Lucy George
Illustrated by Claudia Venturini

Tick Tock

What is synthetic phonics?

Synthetic phonics teaches children to recognise the sounds of letters and to blend (synthesise) them together to make whole words.

Understanding sound/letter relationships gives children the confidence and ability to read unfamiliar words, without having to rely on memory or guesswork; this helps them progress towards independent reading.

Did you know? Spoken English uses more than 40 speech sounds. Each sound is called a *phoneme*. Some phonemes relate to a single letter (d-o-g) and others to combinations of letters (sh-ar-p). When a phoneme is written down it is called a *grapheme*. Teaching these sounds, matching them to their written form and sounding out words for reading is the basis of synthetic phonics.

Consultant

I love reading phonics has been created in consultation with language expert Abigail Steel. She has a background in teaching and teacher training and is a respected expert in the field of Synthetic Phonics. Abigail Steel is a regular contributor to educational publications. Her international education consultancy supports parents and teachers in the promotion of literacy skills.

Reading tips

This book focuses on the sound:
er as in 'term'

Tricky words in this book

Any words in bold may have unusual spellings or are new and have not yet been introduced.

Tricky words in this book:

aimed their zoom first Earth saw iceberg ocean parked what day like care

Extra ways to have fun with this book

• After the reader has read the story, ask them questions about what they have just read:

What did Hermie do on Earth?
What did Ernie do on Earth?

• Make flashcards of the focus graphemes. Ask the reader to say the sounds. This will help reinforce letter/sound matches.

This story is out of this world!

A pronunciation guide

This grid contains the sounds used in
the story and a guide on how to say them.

s as in sat	a as in ant	t as in tin	p as in pig	i as in ink
n as in net	c as in cat	e as in egg	h as in hen	r as in rat
m as in mug	d as in dog	g as in get	o as in ox	u as in up
l as in log	f as in fan	b as in bag	j as in jug	v as in van
w as in wet	z as in zip	y as in yet	k as in kit	qu as in quick
x as in box	ff as in off	ll as in ball	ss as in kiss	zz as in buzz
ck as in duck	pp as in puppy	nn as in bunny	rr as in arrow	gg as in egg
dd as in daddy	bb as in chubby	tt as in attic	sh as in shop	ch as in chip
th as in thin	th as in the	ng as in sing	nk as in sunk	le as in bottle
ai as in rain	ee as in feet	ie as in pies	oa as in oak	ue as in cue
ar as in park	er as in term			

Be careful not to add an 'uh' sound to 's', 't', 'p',
'c', 'h', 'r', 'm', 'd', 'g', 'l', 'f' and 'b'. For example,
say 'fff' not 'fuh' and 'sss' not 'suh'.

Hermie and Ernie **aimed their** ships. **Zoom!**

It was their **first** trip to **Earth**!

From the ship they **saw** herds of elk and oxen.

They passed an **iceberg** and boats on the **ocean**!

Ernie landed his ship by the kerb with a jump.

Hermie **parked** hers with a jerk.

They went along the kerb,
quick and alert.

What to do for a **day** on Earth?

Hermie wanted a perm.

Her perm was very perky!

"I think you look **like** a twerp!"
Ernie said.

"Buzz off!" she said.

Hermie did not **care**!

Ernie got in the queue for
the opera.

He perched and sang along!

"You can not sing!" Hermie cried.
Ernie did not care!

Hermie and Ernie loved it on Earth,

'It's been a blast!'

Time for take off! They raced back.

Ernie sang opera all the way...
Hermie put her fingers in her ears!

OVER **48** TITLES IN SIX LEVELS
Abigail Steel recommends...

Other titles to enjoy from Level 3

Bart's Go-Cart

978-1-84898-552-0

Queen Ella's Feet

978-1-84898-398-4

Puff Flies

978-1-84898-399-1

Some titles from Level 1

Bad Rat

978-1-84898-277-2

The Best Gift

978-1-84898-396-0

Clint and Grant Play I-Spy

978-1-84898-548-3

Gran and Bret's Trip

978-1-84898-547-6

Some titles from Level 2

Wish Fish

978-1-84898-386-1

Chuck and Duck

978-1-84898-387-8

Pink Bunny

978-1-84898-550-6

Let's go to the Swings

978-1-84898-549-0

An Hachette UK Company
www.hachette.co.uk

Copyright © Octopus Publishing Group Ltd 2012
First published in Great Britain in 2012 by TickTock, a division of Octopus Publishing Group Ltd,
Endeavour House, 189 Shaftesbury Avenue, London WC2H 8JY.
www.octopusbooks.co.uk

ISBN 978 1 84898 557 5

Printed and bound in China
10 9 8 7 6 5 4 3 2 1